The
Angel
Doll

Books by Jerry Bledsoe

The World's Number One, Flat-Out, All-Time
Great Stock Car Racing Book, *1975*
You Can't Live on Radishes, *1976*
Just Folks, *1980*
Where's Mark Twain When We
Really Need Him? *1982*
Carolina Curiosities, *1984*
From Whalebone to Hothouse, *1986*
Bitter Blood, *1988*
Country Cured, *1989*
North Carolina Curiosities, *1990*
The Bare-Bottomed Skier, *1990*
Blood Games, *1991*
Blue Horizons, *1993*
Before He Wakes, *1994*
The Angel Doll, *1996*

The
Angel
Doll

A Christmas Story

Jerry Bledsoe

St. Martin's Press ✇ *New York*

For my brothers, Larry and Phil.

And to the memory of W.C. "Mutt" Burton,
who loved Christmas as few others ever have.

Library of Congress Cataloging-in-Publication Data

Bledsoe, Jerry.
    The angel doll / Jerry Bledsoe.
        p.   cm.
    ISBN 0-312-17104-8
    1. Dolls—Fiction.   2. North Carolina—Fiction.
 3. Christmas stories. 1csh.   I. Title.
 [PS3552.L4178A82   1997]
 813'.54—DC21   97-23595
                                                CIP

First published in the United States by
Down Home Press

First Edition: November 1997

10 9 8 7 6 5 4 3 2 1

*To love for the sake of
being loved is human,
but to love for the sake of
loving is angelic.*

Alphonse DeLamartine

1

Two weeks before Christmas each year, I climb to the high shelf in the storage room and fetch down the big cardboard box secured with tape. "Christmas decorations—sentimental," it says, in black marker ink across the top.

I dust it off, handling it carefully, and deliver it and its precious contents to my wife. She does all of the Christmas decorating at our house

because I long ago proved to be without talent for decorating of any kind
and much too clumsy to deal with the
delicate items involved at Christmas.

After I have hauled in the tree
and erected it in a reasonably straight
fashion, *Linda* opens the box and
begins lifting out its contents: big red
ribbons from a wreath she made
for the door of our small apartment
the first Christmas we spent together;
a handful of glass ornaments, cheap
and chipped, from our first tree; a
small card box containing angels,
snowmen and reindeer that our son,
now grown and living far away, cut
from construction paper to hang on
the tree when he was six; a tiny teddy

bear, minus one ear and an eye, its fur as mangy as a cur's, that Santa brought in pristine condition to our son on his first Christmas; a small, antique, hand-carved creche, a family heirloom that Linda's grandmother handed down before her death.

Finally, she digs into a mass of white tissue paper in the bottom of the box and removes the doll. It is a big, bulky doll, nearly three feet tall, with pink rubber skin, curly blond hair, and huge blue eyes with long black lashes that close when she is laid on her back. The doll is attired in a flow-ing white gown, now slightly brittle and yellowed with age, that reaches to her chubby pink feet, and her jointed *legs can be adjusted so that she can stand on her own.*

The wings must be unfolded carefully, lest they lose their shape. They were constructed of stiff wire, covered in the same sheer white fabric as the gown, and edged in sequins of sparkly gold. The wings are attached to two wires sewn into the back of the gown, but the halo is separate, also made of wire wrapped in gold trim. The long straight wire that holds it above the doll's head connects to a hook imbedded beneath her golden curls where the wires that support the wings also fasten. Attaching the halo is my job. I usually cock it at a rakish angle over her right eye.

4

After Linda has finished her decorating, and the colorful lights are blinking gaily on the tree, I make my lone, annual contribution to the seasonal ritual. I put the angel doll in her place of honor beside the tree, a tangible memory from an unforgettable Christmas nearly half a century earlier.

2

I was ten that year, and never before had Christmas come so agonizingly slowly. My dream was that it would bring me a bicycle. My parents had insisted that I could not have a bike until I was ten, old enough to ride safely, and here I was, months past ten and still no bike.

I was too worldly by then to buy into the Santa thing, of course, although I kept up the facade for the sake of my younger brother, a desperate believer. At seven I had sneaked from bed and secretly watched my parents spreading the presents beneath the tree. I realized from that point that they had to pay for the gifts that Santa brought, and I knew what a serious strain on the family finances a bicycle would be. My father made only forty-five dollars a week driving a truck for a wholesale candy company, and the best that Christmas had brought me had been a Hopalong Cassidy cowboy suit with six-shooter cap busters for each skinny hip—far less costly than a bike.

But with a bicycle, I had pointed out many times to my parents, I could get a paper route of my own. Next summer, when I turned eleven, I would be old enough to get a route with one of the dailies that came into our little town. If I could get such a route and build it up, I told them, I could make ten or twelve dollars a week, big money for an eleven-year-old in Thomasville, North Carolina, in the early fifties.

I already had a paper route of sorts. Half of one anyway. I shared it with my best friend Whitey Black. Whitey's real name was Jimmy, but his fine blond hair was so fair that it appeared almost white, especially under the summer sun, thus the nickname; that and the fact that we found it immensely funny to call somebody named Black "Whitey." Every Tuesday and Thursday, Whitey and I delivered *The Thomasville Tribune* on foot to twenty-six subscribers each on the west side of town. A subscription to the *Tribune* cost ten cents a week, and on the weeks when we could collect from everybody, which were rare, we each showed a profit of a dollar and thirty cents. But we could see a cowboy movie with a cartoon, the *Movietone News*, and a serial to boot at the Davidson Theater for just nine cents; a twelve-ounce RC Cola—belly washers, we called them—cost but a nickel at Noah Ledford's store in my neighborhood, and a *major treat, a vanilla milkshake at the Milky Way out on the National Highway, was only fifteen cents.*

Even our shared paper route had not been easily come by; competition was as fierce for Tribune routes as it was for any others. But the Tribune allowed boys to have routes when they were ten, a year younger than the dailies. The Tribune was published on an ancient flatbed press in the back of an old brick building downtown. The previous spring, when I was still nine, I had started hanging around the press room, hoping to make enough of an impression to land a route by my birthday. That was how I had gotten to know Whitey.

3

Whitey was new to Thomasville. He had come to our town the previous fall with his mother, his younger sister, Sandra, and a man who lived with them but was not his father, I was later to learn. They had settled in a shabby rental house beside the tracks of a railroad feeder line in a rundown part of town. Behind the house was a huge lumber yard for one of Thomasville's big furniture factories.

My friends and I often sneaked off to play in the lumber yard, climbing on the huge stacks of oak and cherry boards and jumping from one to another the way the cowboys leaped from the balconies of saloons in the movies we loved.

The man who lived with Whitey's mother had not remained long. "He drank, and he was mean," Whitey told me later, and said no more. Whitey's father, I eventually discovered, had died in a car wreck when Whitey was six.

My first encounter with Whitey had come not long after the man who lived with his mother had left, and it was painful for both of us, something

14

we never mentioned. I belonged to a Cub Scout pack that met in a club-house in Billy Barnes' back yard. Billy's mom was the den mother. She was a woman with a sweet smile, a kind disposition, and a powerful need to perform good deeds. Each fall she rallied us to go door-to-door gathering canned goods, used clothing and items to be taken to needy families before Thanksgiving. These we delivered on a Saturday morning in a small caravan of neighborhood cars driven by Cub Scout fathers.

One of our stops the year before had been at Whitey's house. Whitey's mother answered Mrs. Barnes' knock. She seemed surprised *but pleased to find us standing there on the small, sagging porch with our boxes of goods and our beams of goodwill. She was a tall, bony woman with long, lank hair, hollow cheeks, deeply set blue eyes and a look of perpetual weariness. As Mrs. Barnes attempted to make small talk with her, Whitey's little sister came to the door and stood clinging to her mother's dress. She was four then, tiny and frail, with the same fair skin and light hair as Whitey. Her right leg was shriveled and encased in a heavy steel brace that she propelled forward only with extreme effort. These were the years of the great polio epidemic, and Whitey's mother had already been*

forced to face our own parents' greatest fear.

"Why, hello, sweetheart, what's
your name?" Mrs. Barnes said cheer-
ily, but the child hid her face behind
her mother's leg.

"Say 'I'm Sandy,'" Whitey's
mother prompted. "Can't you say
hello to the nice lady?"

But the girl only buried her
face deeper into her mother's skirt.
"She's shy. Aren't you, honey?"
Whitey's mother said apologetically.

For a moment, we all stood
awkwardly on the porch.

"Won't y'all come in?"
Whitey's mother said, breaking the
silence.

"We've got to be going," Mrs. Barnes quickly responded. "We've got other stops to make. We just wanted to leave these things and wish you a happy Thanksgiving."

"Well, that's so nice of y'all," Whitey's mother said. She turned then and called inside the house, "Jimmy, come and help these good people."

Whitey had come with obvious reluctance, clearly embarrassed, his gaze never rising off the floor. "Look at all the nice things they've brought us," his mother said. "Help them with it, Jimmy."

He stepped out and snatched the box of canned and packaged foods that I was holding, turned abruptly *and disappeared inside. His shame, humiliation and resentment were so apparent that I knew instantly that if I ever felt the urge to commit charity again, it would be from a distance— and anonymously.*

4

After that first encounter with Whitey, I occasionally saw him from afar at Main Street School where I was in the fourth grade class of Miss Clara Cox, a prim and proper spinster who resided with her aging mother. But if he noticed me, he never showed it. Although he was only a few months younger than I, he was a grade behind me, and we had no opportunities to meet until the spring, when we both

began going to the *Tribune* after
school on Tuesdays and Thursdays.
Even then, we avoided one another,
never speaking.

The circulation manager of the
Tribune, a former Thomasville Bull-
dogs football player in his early
twenties, was once a paper boy him-
self. He would sometimes pay a quar-
ter to boys who helped put inserts in
the fat Thursday papers, and there
was never a shortage of eager volun-
teers, myself and Whitey included.
One day he picked Whitey and me,
and we found ourselves working
beside one another. While we labored,
intent on being quick and competent,
an older carrier who was always

fomenting trouble reached across my back unbeknownst to me and gave Whitey a sharp jab on his shoulder, then returned instantly and innocently to his work.

Whitey turned on me angrily. "Don't do that again," he said.

"Do what?"

"You know what."

"I didn't do anything," I protested.

"Keep 'em moving, boys," called the circulation manager over the roar of the press, from which he was bringing another armload of papers. "No time for squabbling."

Just as we were getting back into the rhythm of the work, the mis-

chievous carrier gave Whitey another shot, this one throwing him off balance.

Next thing I knew, Whitey was on top of me and we were grappling and yelling on the floor.

Suddenly, strong hands grabbed each of us by a shoulder and yanked us apart.

"No fighting in here!" the circulation manager commanded.

"He started it," Whitey said defiantly.

"I did not."

"What's this about?" asked the circulation manager, holding us apart by the scruff of the neck.

"He hit me," Whitey said.

"I didn't either," I protested.

The older carrier who had started it all laughed, and the circulation manager fired a stern glance his way.

"Hey, don't look at me," said the older boy, holding up his hands. "I don't know nothing about it."

"We're not going to have any rowdy stuff around here," the circulation manager proclaimed, glancing at the older carrier as he said it. "Now I want you two to apologize to one another."

Neither of us said anything.

"Go ahead," the circulation manager said with force enough to make it an order.

"I'm sorry," we both mumbled.

"Now shake hands."

We reached out tentatively for a brief grasp.

"That's better," he said. "Now let me tell you something."

I braced myself for a lecture of admonition, certain that my dream of a paper route had just vanished. Instead, I heard him saying, "I'm going to have a route opening next week, and if you two think you can get along, I'll consider letting you share it. What do you say to that?"

At first, I could hardly believe my ears, but I heard Whitey mutter, "I can get along with him," and I quickly agreed, "Me, too."

5

Get along we did. The next week we started our route, carrying our papers in big canvas bags draped from our small shoulders. We walked together to the start of the route and waited for one another at the end, sometimes stopping at Noah Ledford's store on the way home to buy penny candies. By summer, we had become close friends and spent as much time together as we could. We caught min-

nows and crawfish in the big creek at the foot of my street, made slingshots and broke bottles with the small stones we fired at them, played baseball in the empty lot beside Shirley Pierce's house (Whitey was a good hitter and a fast runner), camped one night in pup tents in Billy's back yard after roasting hot dogs and marshmallows over an open fire.

Whitey did not get to play as often as I and my other friends did, however. Usually, his mother had things for him to do at home. Or he stayed to keep company with his little sister, who was often sick, rarely got out and apparently had no other friends or companions.

Whitey never invited anybody to his house. He was embarrassed, I later realized, by its sparse and worn furnishings and his mother's lackadaisical housekeeping, and didn't want anybody to discover that his family survived on handouts and monthly checks from county services. But as we grew closer, I began to stop by his house occasionally. Gradually I was accepted inside.

Whitey had his own room (I was envious; I had to share mine with my brother Larry), where he kept his few prized possessions: his baseball glove (he was a lefty), a couple of model airplanes he'd built, a small collection of lead soldiers and a few

29

comic books (*Captain Marvel* and
Scrooge McDuck were his favorites).
His sister slept on a small cot pushed
into a corner of her mother's room,
over which was hung a picture, cut
from a calendar, of an angel standing
guard over a circle of children.

Sandy, I soon discovered, was
fascinated with angels. Whitey often
read to her, and I had gone with him
several times to our town's small
library on the second floor of the city
hall in search of books to read to
Sandy. He had long since exhausted
the entire stock of angel books. Her
favorite was called *The Littlest Angel*,
and she had her own copy. A Sunday
school class had brought it in a box of

gifts and food the previous Christmas.

*"She knows it by heart,"
Whitey told me, "but she still wants
me to read it to her."*

*One Thursday just before
school was to resume after summer
vacation, Whitey and I finished our
paper route early and hurried to his
house to pick up his glove so that we
could join a late baseball game of
older boys that still lacked a few
players. I could tell when Whitey
asked permission that his mother was
not pleased.*

*"You haven't spent any time at
all with your sister today," she said.*

*"Jimmy, read to me just a little
before you go," Sandy pleaded.*

"Can I go after I read?" Jimmy asked, casting me a glance that begged forbearance.

"Just go on before you drive me crazy," his mother said.

"No, I want to read first," Whitey said, and Sandy's face erupted in smile.

Sandy fetched *The Littlest Angel* and nestled close to her brother on the soiled and sagging sofa as he opened the book.

"He's the same age as me, ain't he Jimmy?" she said.

"And he has freckles just like yours, too," he added.

She giggled at the Littlest Angel's misadventures in Heaven, and

laughed out loud when his halo,
which kept drooping over his right
eye, fell off completely and rolled down
one of Heaven's golden streets.

"He's funny," she said.

When Whitey got to the part in
the story where a child was to be born
in Bethlehem, and all the other angels
in Heaven were vying to find the finest
gifts to bestow upon Him, and the
Littlest Angel was despairing that he
had only his humble treasures from
Earth to offer—a dried butterfly, the
shell of a robin's egg, two smooth
pebbles from a creek—Sandy inter-
rupted.

"What would you give Him,
Jimmy?"

Whitey paused, thinking. "I don't know, my baseball glove, I guess. What would you give?"

"My book," she said without hesitation.

Whitey went on to finish the story, reading how the Lord chose the Littlest Angel's gift over all the others and turned it into the star of Bethlehem.

"Jimmy, will I be an angel?" Sandy asked as he was closing the book.

"You already are," he said, leaning over to kiss her forehead. Her face could have brightened the darkest sky.

6

*T*homasville ushered in Christmas
each year with a big parade down
Main Street that always featured Miss
America (don't ask me how my little
town managed that) and ended with
Santa Claus sitting high in a little red
sleigh pulled by eight papier-mache
reindeer. This year the Santa float was
towed by a new tractor from the Ford
place, driven by a dour man in a
toboggan with a cigarette dangling

from his lips. Santa tossed handfuls of
hard candies wrapped in cellophane
to children along the way. He was
tailed by a police car with the dome
light flashing and a gang of boys
scrambling madly for the goodies.
Whitey and I both ended up with our
pockets stuffed.

I loved the Christmas season
better than any other. I couldn't get
enough of the festive lights that were
strung across downtown streets, the
wreaths and candy canes that draped
every light post, the animated Christ-
mas scenes in the windows at Belk's
Department Store, the sugar cookies
in the shapes of bells and Christmas
trees at Tasty Bakery, the notices in

the newspaper of how many more shopping days were left. There was a palpable air of excitement, especially on Saturdays when the downtown stores filled with shoppers and Christmas carols rent the air even on the sidewalks.

I had already decided what I was buying everybody that year with the money I'd saved: for my daddy a fishing tackle box; for my mother a bottle of Evening in Paris perfume (a sales clerk at McLellan's Five & Dime had sprayed some on my wrist and never had I smelled anything so sweet and wonderful); for my brother Larry, who was two and a half years younger, a football; for my baby brother Phil, a late arrival, who was just eighteen months old, a toy dump truck. Whitey was with me when I exhausted my savings with the purchase of the dump truck.

"What are you getting for Sandy?" I asked him.

"I don't know," he said. "She wants an angel doll, but I can't find one."

In the coming days, Whitey and I prowled every store in Thomasville searching for an angel doll. We found angel figurines, angel ornaments, framed cheap prints of angels, but no angel dolls. And no clerk in any store could recall ever seeing one. We couldn't even find one

*in the fat Sears & Roebuck catalog that
my mother kept at our house. Still
Whitey remained determined. One
way or another, he vowed, he would
get Sandy an angel doll.*

*On a Thursday afternoon,
nearly three weeks before Christmas,
Whitey and I were on our way to the
Tribune building to pick up our
papers when he suddenly stopped in
front of McLellan's Five & Dime and
stood staring at the display window.
When I looked to see what had
grabbed his attention and was holding him so transfixed, I saw the angel
doll for the first time—but she wasn't
an angel then. She was standing
amidst a group of dolls, the biggest*

and prettiest of the bunch. She was
wearing a frilly pink dress, two pink
ribbons in her blond hair, and pink
fringed socks with her white shoes. A
small pink and white purse was
fastened to one wrist.

"I wonder if somebody could
take a regular doll and make it into an
angel," Whitey said.

"I bet Billy's mom could," I told
him. "She's got an electric sewing
machine and she makes all kinds of
things."

That planted the seed in
Whitey's brain, and it blossomed
immediately. By the time we got to the
Tribune office, he had decided that we
should go and talk with Mrs. Barnes

as soon as we finished our route.

And that we did.

Whitey explained it all in an excited voice, then stood waiting anxiously for an answer as Billy's mom thought about it.

"I don't see why we couldn't do it," she finally said. "The only problem would be the wings and the halo, but I probably could fashion those from wire. I've got some material here that would be fine for the gown, and for covering the wings too. I'd just need to get some sequins or something to pretty it up."

"What would you charge me?" Whitey asked.

"Why, honey, I wouldn't

charge a thing in the world."

"I want to pay," Whitey put in quickly and firmly.

"Okay...well we can work that out."

Mrs. Barnes decided that it might be better for her to go and look at the doll before Whitey bought it, just to see what problems she might encounter. She thought that she could do it the next morning while we were in school.

As soon as school was out on Friday, Whitey and I headed for Billy's house. Mrs. Barnes must have seen us coming, for she greeted us at the door.

"Did you get to go see the

doll?" Whitey asked.

"I sure did, honey," she said, "and she's going to make a beautiful angel."

7

I'd never seen Whitey so happy. He wanted to go right then to buy the doll, but he didn't have his money with him and we both still had subscribers on our route from whom we needed to collect that week. The stores downtown were staying open now until nine on Friday and Saturday nights, so we had plenty of time. Since we were closer to Whitey's house than to our paper route, we decided to go first to his house to get his money, then collect from our customers before going downtown to buy the doll.

Whitey's mother was in a foul mood. We both sensed it as soon as we entered the house and headed for his room.

"Where do you think you're going?" she called from a chair close to the kerosene heater where she sat reading a magazine and smoking a cigarette. She was the only woman I'd ever seen smoke a cigarette.

We both stopped and Whitey turned to face her. "I've got to go to my room for a minute," he told her. "Then we've got to go finish collecting from our route. And I've got a few other things I need to do."

"Well, I've got things I need for you to be doing here, too," she said.

"Mama, I've got to do this," he told her with an edge to his voice. "I can do whatever you want me to do later."

Nothing more was said, and we continued on to his room and closed the door. He made me stand facing the door with my eyes closed while he got his money from its secret hiding place. I heard him rustling about before he said, "Okay, you can turn around now."

His money was in an old sock, and he emptied it onto his bed and counted it: seven worn dollar bills, four

*half dollars, six quarters, thirteen
dimes, twelve nickels and forty-three
pennies. Twelve dollars and eighty-
three cents. The doll was eight-ninety-
nine. With tax it would be nine-
eighteen. Whitey rolled the bills
tightly, wrapped them with a rubber
band and stuck them in his jacket
pocket. He poured two dollars and a
half in coins into a pocket of his jeans.
The rest he put back into the sock, and
while I faced the door again, he returned it to its hiding place.*

*"You could at least go speak to
your sister," his mother said when we
emerged from the room.*

*I waited outside while Whitey
went to see Sandy.*

"She's sick again," he told me when he came out.

We split up when we got to our route so that we could make our collections quicker, agreeing to meet at the starting point. From there, we would go to McLellan's to buy the doll. Whitey didn't have as many customers to collect from as I did, but when I got to the starting point, with an extra seventy cents jangling in my pocket, he wasn't there.

Ten minutes...fifteen minutes...a half hour later, Whitey still hadn't shown up. The sun was beginning to set and I was growing concerned. After another fifteen minutes, I set out in search of him. I'd gotten no more than a block before I saw him coming around the corner. Relieved, I waved to him. As he came closer, I saw the frantic look on his face.

"What's the matter?" I asked.

"I lost my money," he said.

At first, it didn't register.

"What money?"

"The dollar bills I put in my jacket pocket," he said and burst into tears. "The money I was going to use to buy the doll."

I hadn't seen Whitey cry before, and I didn't know how to react.

"Maybe we can find it," I said.

"I already looked," he said, snuffling, trying to quell his emotion.

"How did you lose it?"

"I don't know. It just slipped out of my pocket, I guess. I reached to check on it and it wasn't there."

"Where were you then?"

"I was just leaving Mrs. Bell's house."

"Well, that's where we've got to start," I said. "We'll retrace every step. Come on."

We ran all the way to Mrs. Bell's house to begin the search and backtracked from there. Whitey remembered that the money was still in his pocket when we passed Noah Ledford's store, because he had checked then, so we didn't have to go all the way back to his house. We searched along sidewalks, in yards, in

51

gutters and ditches, under bushes, in street drains and dead flower beds, all to no avail.

"I won't be able to get the doll now," Whitey said. His face was the picture of despair.

"Don't worry," I told him. "It'll turn up. We need to go to every house you collected from and ask if anybody found it."

It was well after dark when we finished that. Nobody had seen the money, but if they did come across it, all had promised, they'd hold it for Whitey.

"We need a flashlight," Whitey said.

"My daddy has one," I told

him. "We can go get it."

I knew that my mother would be worried sick already that I hadn't come home yet, and if I didn't get there soon, she'd probably have the police looking for me. Her worry had blown into a fury by the time we got to my house.

"You could at least have let me know where you were," she stormed. But when I explained the situation, she softened. We couldn't go back out without eating, she insisted, but Whitey didn't want to take the time, so she made pork chop biscuits to send with us while my dad fetched one flashlight from a kitchen drawer and another from his truck.

When we came outside, nibbling at our biscuits, my dad had the car cranked and told us to get in.

"I'll take you around there," he said. "The car will give more light."

An hour later, we had made another complete circuit of the route and still hadn't found the money. My hands and feet were numb from the cold, my nose red and runny, my ears tingling.

"I don't think you're going to find it tonight, boys," my dad told us. "Let's go on home and you can look again tomorrow."

But Whitey didn't want to go. Unable to dissuade him, we left him there with one of my daddy's flash-

lights, a tiny, dejected figure, trudging along forlornly, thrusting a frail shaft of yellow hope into the darkness.

8

I was sitting at the dinette eating a
bowl of oatmeal with my brothers
Saturday morning when I heard a
clamor on our front porch. My mother
went to see what it was. When she
opened the door, I could hear Whitey
shouting, "I found it! I found it!"
He was so breathless with excitement
that he hardly could explain what had
happened.

He had continued his search

*until nearly ten-thirty the evening
before, then had gone home to a night
of worry and fitful sleep. But when he
got up and dressed this morning to
renew the hunt, he had felt an unfa-
miliar lump in the back of his jacket.
Something was trapped inside the
lining. He checked the pocket then and
discovered a hole in the back, one he
wouldn't normally feel when he put
his hand inside. He worked the lump
toward the hole, and out popped the
money.*

*"I was toting it back there all
the time we were looking for it," he
said with a happy laugh.*

*"Where is it now?" my mother
asked.*

"Right here," he said, patting the pocket of his jeans.

"You don't have a hole in that pocket, do you?"

"No ma'am," he said with a chuckle. "I checked."

"Well, please don't lose it again," she chided.

"Don't worry," he told her.

We left for McLellan's as soon as I finished my oatmeal and hot chocolate. The stores had just opened for the day, but it was Saturday and Christmas was near, and already the streets were getting crowded.

We ran the last few hundred feet to the store, dodging the early shoppers, skidding to a halt at the

McLellan's window. Whitey's face suddenly dropped.

"It's gone," he said.

I trailed behind as he bolted for the door and headed for the toy section in a frantic dash.

"Excuse me," he said in an anxious and eager voice to the woman behind the toy counter, "but there was a big doll in the window the other day, had on a pink dress...."

"Yes," said the woman, "that was the only one we had like that."

"Did somebody buy it?" Whitey asked, his voice tremulous.

"I'm not sure," said the woman. "A lady came to look at it yesterday morning and we took it out of the *window for her. I thought she might come back for it so I put it under the counter. I didn't work last night, so I don't know if she came or not. Somebody else might have bought it."*

"Could you look?" Whitey asked.

"Sure."

The woman walked the length of the counter, her head bent in search, before squatting out of sight.

"Oh, here she is," I heard her say, and when she reappeared she had the doll in her arms.

"I want to buy it," Whitey said quickly.

"She's expensive," the woman said, eyeing him appraisingly.

"I've got the money," Whitey told her, producing the roll of bills.

"She sure is a pretty thing," the woman said later, as she was boxing the doll in tissue paper. "Somebody's going to be awfully happy this Christmas."

"I know she is," Whitey said.

9

After Whitey and I had dropped the doll off with Mrs. Barnes and returned to my house, my dad asked Whitey if his mother had gotten their Christmas tree yet.

"No, not yet," Whitey said.

"You want to go with us to get one?" my dad asked. Whitey accepted eagerly, but said he needed to go home first to tell his mother where he was going. We left right after lunch *and stopped to pick up Whitey on the way.*

We drove out into the country-side to a farm owned by relatives who let us cut our Christmas tree there every year. We stopped first at the big, tin-roofed white house to visit for a while. Then we piled back into the car and followed a rutted tractor road through a pasture gate to a big field of sedge, wild blackberry vines and young cedars that stretched up a hillside to the edge of the woods. There must have been a thousand potential Christmas trees there, and Whitey, my brother and I ran from one to another, our clothing gathering hitchhiker burrs and beggar's lice as we went, assessing each before making our choices.

Larry and I picked a plump one nearly seven feet tall, because it had a bird's nest hidden in its branches. Whitey chose a shorter and thinner one. So intoxicated were we by the excitement of the moment and the wondrous fresh fragrance of cedar that we hardly noticed the scratches inflicted on our hands by the trees' prickly needles as we dragged them back to the car and loaded them into the trunk.

My dad had brought his .22 rifle, and after the trees were loaded we went into the woods and searched out a familiar oak tree, its upper branches laden with mistletoe. My dad let Whitey and me fire a few rounds each at the parasitic clumps before the expense of wasted shells caused him to take back the rifle and knock down a big clump with his first shot. On the way back to the car, we stopped at a holly grove and loaded our arms with red-berried boughs.

Late that afternoon, my dad nailed the tree to a platform he'd hammered together and removed his favorite chair from the living room so that he could erect the tree in the front window. It seemed to fill the whole room. My mother got out the decorations and spent the first half hour changing bulbs, trying to get the strands of lights to burn. The bubble lights, my favorites, sprang to life without protest and soon were dancing merrily. After my mother had strung the lights, we all joined in hanging the ornaments and wrapping the tree in gold and silver garland. Larry and I added the finishing touches, helped on the lower branches by our baby brother. We gobbed the tree with cotton balls of make-believe snow, draped it in tinsel icicles and swathed it in filmy angel hair. It was a vision when we'd finished, truly a sight to behold. Our front window blazed in the early darkness.

"Doesn't seem like Christmas until the tree's up," my mother ob-

served.

It didn't seem to me that Christmas ever would come. A week passed, the longest of my life thus far, but even slower days lay ahead, for we still had nine days to go. As I was cutting through Billy's yard on my way to school Monday, his mom stopped me and told me she had finished the doll the night before. Would I mind telling Whitey?

I didn't see him until after school, and he couldn't wait to get to Billy's house. We trotted all the way. Mrs. Barnes brought the doll from her sewing room, fussing with the halo.

"It may be a little trouble for your sister to keep this on her," she

said, bending the wire slightly to straighten the glittery circle over the doll's head.

"That's all right," Whitey said with a little smile. "She knows about that."

Mrs. Barnes held the doll out in front of her.

"Well, what do you think?"

For a moment, Whitey just stared, saying nothing, as if in awe.

"It looks just like an angel," he said.

"Oh, good," Mrs. Barnes said. "Then I didn't do so bad after all."

"Oh, no ma'am, you did fine," Whitey said. "She's beautiful."

"Well, I was a little worried

about these wings," she said. "I was afraid that they would just pull the gown up in front and droop down behind, and that's exactly what they did until I put this little hook back here." She turned the doll to show the hook at the base of the neck where the wires in the gown attached.

"The hair hides it, so I don't think anybody will notice that," she said.

"I don't think so," Whitey agreed. "How much do I owe you?"

"Well, I know a woman who's a doll collector, and she told me she would buy the outfit this doll was wearing, if you want to sell it, and that would more than cover the cost of the material."

"That would be okay," Whitey said.

"It really didn't take too much time once I decided how to do the wings and halo," Mrs. Barnes went on, "so I thought maybe a dollar would do it. Is that too much?"

"No," Whitey said. "Are you sure that's enough?"

"Yes, it's plenty."

"I'll have to go home and get the money," Whitey told her.

"You can just drop it off any-time," Mrs. Barnes replied.

"Would you mind keeping her here until Christmas Eve?" Whitey asked. "I don't want Sandy to see her."

"I wouldn't mind at all," Mrs. Barnes said. "To tell the truth, I've come to enjoy her company."

10

As we went to pick up our papers on Tuesday, Whitey told me that Sandy was worse and the doctor had been to see her. He said he would have to hurry home after he had finished his part of the route, and he didn't wait for me as usual. I didn't get to talk to him again until Thursday. He looked worried. Sandy still hadn't improved.

"The doctor said he might have to put her in the hospital," Whitey

said, "but she don't want to go."

This was collection day, and today's paper would be the last before Christmas, which would be the coming Tuesday. All the carriers were filled with anticipation about the Christmas tips they might get. The prospect even brightened Whitey's mood.

The papers were thick with ads, and we struggled under their weight, but the reward was ample. Three different subscribers gave me full dollar tips—one a shiny silver dollar. My pocket was heavy with quarters and half dollars. One woman handed me a full pound of chocolate covered cherries, and it took all the resolve I could muster to keep from ripping into them right then. Already I was scheming how I could keep them hidden from my brothers.

Whitey did well too. He got four dollar tips, and one woman gave him a beautifully wrapped gift that he couldn't wait to open. He tore into it as we headed home. Inside was a new pair of gloves and a cap with ear flaps lined with rabbit fur.

School let out at noon on Friday for the holidays. Eleven blessed days without classroom tedium lay ahead of us. Whitey and I went to finish collecting our route after school. I thought we might go prowling through the stores uptown afterward, *but he couldn't tarry. He had to get home and help look after Sandy, he said.*

I didn't see Whitey all weekend. On Saturday, I had to rehearse for the young people's Christmas pageant at our church, First Methodist. I never really understood why I needed to practice. I was a shepherd again, abiding my flocks by night, and all I had to do was stand there in my daddy's faded bathrobe that smelled of tobacco smoke, holding a staff and beholding the Angel of the Lord, who was played by Betty Jean Smith from my Sunday school class.

The pageant on Sunday night was well attended and warmly re-

*ceived, as it usually was, and after-
ward the congregation joined in
singing carols, and the preacher and
the deacons handed out brown paper
bags filled with fruits, nuts and candies to all the young and elderly.*

*Christmas Eve was my favorite
day of all. I loved the sweet anticipation and excitement it brought. I loved
being downtown and joining in the
last-minute bustle and cheery goodwill, loved hearing people calling
"Merry Christmas!" to one another,
even to strangers. I spent the whole
afternoon downtown, venturing into
practically every store—even poking
my head into the musty, beery pool-
room, the only spot with no sign of*

Christmas evident. I stared wistfully at the blank and silent televisions in the window at Holton Furniture Co. (TV was new then, for us an unobtainable dream. The sets in the window were turned on each evening when our only area station began its snowy broadcasts, and crowds gathered on the sidewalk to watch.) I spent some of my tip money to buy a few extra little gifts for my family, treated myself to a bagful of chocolate covered peanuts at the dime store, and a Cherry Smash at Rexall Drugs, where I whiled away the better part of an hour thumbing through the comic books and reading the cartoons in the Saturday Evening Post. A cartoonist for the Post was *what I hoped to be. Twilight neared and storekeepers began to prepare for closing. It was only with the greatest reluctance and a twinge of sadness that I headed for home just four blocks away on Fifth Avenue. I dared not be late, for as soon as my dad finished work on Christmas Eve, we loaded ourselves into the car and headed across town to an uncle's house for a big family supper and exchange of presents.*

Back at home later, Larry and I cajoled until we were allowed to open the presents that had come in the mail from our grandmother and other relatives in Virginia. My total haul for the evening was far from what I had hoped: a sweater, two pairs of socks, a woolen scarf, a pair of bedroom shoes that I never would wear in this life. My only good present was from my grandmother in Virginia, a book about magic tricks that came with an actual magician's wand. I wanted to try some of the tricks, but my parents insisted that if we were not in bed and asleep within fifteen minutes, Santa would pass us by. That threat panicked my brother to such an extent that he nearly forgot to put out his annual offering to Santa—a peanut butter and banana sandwich. This could be made only on Merita Bread, the bread that sponsored The Lone Ranger on radio. My brother was

*utterly devoted to this show. He could
abide no other sounds while it was on
and affixed his ear to the radio
speaker for the duration of every
broadcast.*

    *I couldn't go to sleep, of course.
I never could on Christmas Eve—didn't
want to either. I pretended sleep long
after my brother had dropped off,
listening intently for any sound that
would indicate a bicycle being rolled
into the house.*

    *I heard my parents talking low
in the living room, and later in their
bedroom adjoining ours, and before
long I picked up the unmistakable
sounds of my father snoring, but I
had heard nothing to indicate that a*

bicycle might be in my immediate future. I began to doubt that it would be.

Usually, I was pretty good at finding my parents' hiding places for Santa toys, but this year I had found nothing. I knew that they couldn't hide a bike in the house, of course. A bike was too big for the car trunk, and my dad's truck was too packed and jumbled with goods to accommodate one. They would have had to stash it at somebody else's house, a neighbor's, perhaps, or a relative's. But I had heard nobody leave the house, and nobody arrive. Clearly, there could be only one explanation: I wasn't getting a bike.

I had known my parents couldn't afford it; it was too much to expect in the first place. Maybe if I took extra jobs and saved my money prudently, I could buy one for myself by summer, a used one, and fix it up. With such dire thoughts, I drifted off to sleep.

"Hey...hey...wake up."

I vaguely heard the voice and realized my brother was punching me. I stirred to darkness and confusion. It couldn't have been later than two o'clock.

"Come on," my brother whispered, standing beside the bed, "get up. He's been, he's been."

I crawled groggily from bed,

and tiptoeing as quietly as our cold and creaky, linoleum-covered floors would allow, followed him to the darkened living room. There, in the faint glow filtering through the window from the street light out front, I saw the silhouette of a bicycle, its kickstand down, its front wheel canted, a basket on the handlebars for carrying schoolbooks and newspapers. I could hardly believe my eyes.

My brother was scrambling beneath the tree, stirring a fierce racket. "I think I got a Lone Ranger set!" he called to me, trying to keep his voice low, just as my father's voice boomed from the bedroom: "You boys get back to bed!"

There was no sleeping the rest of that night, of course, no matter how hard I tried. The few hours remaining before daylight dragged on longer than had all the days before Christmas.

By dawn, I was up and dressed and examining my new bike. It was a bright red J.C. Higgins from the Sears and Roebuck catalog, one of the less expensive bikes available, not exactly stylish or prestigious, but to me it was a beauty. I had learned to ride more than a year earlier on the bikes of older boys in the neighborhood, but my mother never quite believed it, and she stood watching from the porch in her housecoat, as I

pushed my new bike into the yard
and climbed aboard for the first time.

"Ple-e-ease be careful," she said.

Soon I was flying down Fifth
Avenue, the cold wind making my
eyes tear and my nose run. Never had
I known such joy. On my second pass
by Billy's house, I saw him rolling a
new Schwinn Black Phantom out his
front door. The Black Phantom was
every boy's dream, the fanciest bike on
the market, but my J.C. Higgins was
lighter and faster. I knew I could
outrun him anytime and soon was
proving it.

It was about mid-morning
before Mrs. Barnes waved us down
and asked me if I'd seen Whitey.

"He didn't come to get the doll," she said. *"I just wonder if something is wrong."*

In my excitement, I hadn't even thought about the doll, hadn't thought about Whitey. I'd go find out, I told her. I wanted to show him my new bike anyway.

I stopped to tell my mother where I was going, and minutes later I turned onto Whitey's street, standing up on the pedals. Two cars were parked in front of his house. That was unusual, but it was Christmas, and I figured his mother must have company. That surely was why Whitey hadn't yet come to get the doll.

I climbed off the bike and

parked it carefully. I'd started for the porch when I saw a small figure far down the railroad tracks, walking alone, his head down, and realized it was Whitey. "Hey, Whitey, wait up!" I called, trotting toward him in the fine cinders along the tracks. He turned, saw me and stopped. As I drew near, I saw that he looked stricken. His eyes were red and swollen.

"What's wrong?" I asked, surprised.

"Sandy died," he said.

His blunt words stunned me. I'd never faced death before. It simply seemed impossible for it to involve somebody I knew, to invade such a joyous time.

"When?" I asked.

"Last night," he said. "We took her to the hospital, but they couldn't do nothing. She told me the angels were coming. She could see 'em. She said, 'Look, Jimmy, look!' But I couldn't see nothing. And then after a little while she just breathed away."

I didn't know what to say or do. I just stood there feeling helpless.

"Her book's gone," he said. "I searched all over, but I can't find it. I wanted to take it to her at the funeral home, but it's not in the house anymore."

"I got a bike," I told him. "You want to ride it?" I couldn't think of anything else to offer.

JERRY BLEDSOE

"*No, I'm just going to walk for a little bit right now. I've got to try to help Mama after while. She's not doing too good.*"

Only then did I realize that I was intruding. "I'm sorry," I told him and turned to go.

I'd walked only a short distance back toward my bike when he called out to me.

"Tell Mrs. Barnes she can take that doll and give it to somebody that can use it," he said. "But you better tell her to put them other clothes back on her. Nobody else probably would want a dumb ol' angel."

11

I couldn't have imagined when I left Whitey on the railroad tracks that day that I never would see him again, but that was how it turned out. He and his mother departed that afternoon to bury Sandy in South Carolina, from where they had come.

When I went to pick up my papers on my new bike two days later, the circulation manager told me I would have to take the whole route because Whitey wouldn't be coming back. It shocked me, but I agreed. With my bike, I finished the whole job in less time than it took to do half of it before.

Somebody must have come to retrieve the belongings that Whitey and his mother had left behind, for their house turned up empty early in the new year. If Whitey had been back, he hadn't let anybody know. I kept thinking that I might hear from him somehow—a letter perhaps—but I never did. I overheard adults saying that Whitey's mother had left so many debts behind that she didn't want anybody to know where she had gone.

The next summer I got a route with the Winston-Salem paper and kept it for five years, even after we'd moved to a bigger house in another neighborhood and I'd gone to work on weekends for fifty-cents an hour at Murphy's Grocery downtown.

I joined the Army after high school and left Thomasville for good. Eventually, I drifted into the newspaper business, married, had a son, settled in a nearby city. I became a columnist and with time wrote a book. One of my first book signings was at a newsstand that had opened in a new shopping center on a hillside just south of Thomasville where my father had always dreamed of building a stone house. Some relatives showed up, along with a few of my old friends from high school.

In the small crowd was a woman whose face I knew I should recognize but didn't. She smiled when she got to the table and said, "Everybody on Fifth Avenue is so proud of you," and I realized then that she was Billy's mom. I stood and hugged her. Billy, she told me, had become a physician and was practicing in Richmond. Her husband, an accountant, had died a few years earlier, and she was alone now.

"I've got something for you," she told me, after I had signed a book for her and another for Billy. "It's out *in the car. Let me go get it."*

In a few minutes, she returned carrying a big box and placed it on the table. I opened it and saw the angel doll. Twenty-five years had passed since she had transformed it.

"He never came back for it," she said. "I kept thinking that he would but he never did. I never could find out where they had moved so that I could send it to him. I've had it all these years. I thought you might want it."

That night I told the story of the angel doll to my wife and son. We carefully packed the doll away, then brought it out at Christmas and put it under our tree for the first time. My son was ten then, getting his first full-

size bike for Christmas. He was a little too old for The Littlest Angel, but I read it to him that Christmas Eve anyway, along with all the other Christmas stories we'd always read. Although he's in his thirties now, I've read it to him every Christmas Eve since as well. If he's ever looked upon it as an ordeal, tolerated for the sake of his foolish and soft-hearted father, he's been too decent to make it known.

12

Years after the angel doll came to reside at our house, I was in a distant city on assignment for a magazine early one December, having breakfast and reading the newspaper in a hotel dining room. A young couple came in and seated themselves at a table near mine. With them was a child, a girl, pale and thin, perhaps four, or five. I paid no particular attention to them until I noticed that the child was clinging to a doll. An angel doll. Then I saw that it was a smaller but almost perfect replica of the doll I soon would be taking from the storage shelf and placing beside our tree.

My gaze was riveted on the doll, and I know the couple must have thought me strange, perhaps even threatening, for I could see them glancing my way and obviously talking about it. Finally, I could repress my curiosity no longer. I got up and approached their table.

"Excuse me," I said, as they looked up warily. "I couldn't help but notice your little girl's doll. I was wondering where you got it. I might like to get one like it."

*"This is our daughter Emily,"
the young man said. The child smiled
shyly, clutching her doll tighter, as if
she were afraid I might try to snatch it
from her.*

*Emily had leukemia, the young
man told me, and was being treated at
a nearby children's hospital. The
nurses there had given her the doll.
Every child at the hospital got one at
Christmastime, he said.*

*Embarrassed, I thanked them,
apologized for intruding, wished
Emily a quick and complete recovery.*

*"Oh, she'll be fine," her mother
said with the confidence that only faith
and deep longing can provide. "The
doctors at the hospital are taking very*

good care of her."

"The doctors and my guardian angel," said Emily, holding up the doll for me to see. "She'll always look after me, won't she, Mommy?"

"That's right, honey," said her mother.

I left the dining room, went straight to the hotel desk and asked directions to the children's hospital. When I got there, I searched out the public relations officer, told her of my experience in the hotel dining room and expressed my curiosity about the angel dolls. Where did they come from?

"I wish I could tell you," she said, "but we don't have the faintest

idea. It's been going on for years, even before I came here. Somebody just sends them every December with instructions to give one to every child. There's always enough."

"I think I know who that might be," I said. "Have you ever heard of a book called The Littlest Angel?"

"I read it as a little girl."

"Well, it all goes back to that," I said, and went on to tell her about Whitey, Sandy and the doll Sandy never got to hold.

Later, back in my hotel room, I searched the telephone directory for Blacks and even called a few who were listed as James, or Jim, or J., but none acknowledged ever living in

Thomasville. I soon realized that even if I found Whitey, I wouldn't know what to say. It was enough to know that he was out there somewhere, that he obviously was doing well, and that he, like I, had learned from our experience so long ago that the gift of Christmas is the gift of love.

Every year now in mid-December, I call the children's hospital.

"Are they there yet?" I ask.

"They're here," the public relations director tells me with a laugh.

I know then that it is time to fetch the tree and bring down from the storage shelf the box marked "Christmas decorations—sentimental."

After Linda has finished her

work, I place the angel doll beside the tree. And as I do, I offer a little wish. "Merry Christmas, Whitey, old friend," I say, "and may she ever bring you love."

The Littlest Angel by Charles Tazewell
was published in 1946 by
the Children's Press.
It remains in print.

1/98   2   1/98
3/00   (5)   1/00